KAMALA HARRIS

FIRST FEMALE VICE PRESIDENT

by Rachel Rose

Consultant: Beth Gambro
Reading Specialist, Yorkville, Illinois

BEARPORT
PUBLISHING

Minneapolis, Minnesota

Teaching Tips

BEFORE READING

- Look at the cover of the book. Discuss the picture and the title.

- Ask readers to brainstorm a list of what they already know about Kamala Harris, including what they learned from the cover. What can they expect to see in this book?

- Go on a picture walk, looking through the pictures to discuss vocabulary and make predictions about the text.

DURING READING

- Read for purpose. Encourage readers to look for key pieces of information they can expect to see in biographies.

- Ask readers to look for the details of the book. What happened to Kamala Harris at different times of her life?

- If readers encounter an unknown word, ask them to look at the sounds in the word. Then, ask them to look at the rest of the page. Are there any clues to help them understand?

AFTER READING

- Encourage readers to pick a buddy and reread the book together.

- Ask readers to name three things Kamala Harris has done throughout her life. Go back and find the pages that tell about these things.

- Ask readers to write or draw something they learned about Kamala Harris.

Credits:
Cover and title page ©Pictorial Press Ltd/Alamy; 3, ©Mark Makela/Getty Images; 5, ©Bloomberg /Getty Images; 7, ©Jim Heaphy/Wikimedia; 8, ©Kelvin Sterling Scott/iStock; 11, ©MediaNews Group/East Bay Times/Getty Images; 12, ©Policeguy31/Wikimedia; 13, ©Jim West/Alamy; 15, ©Aaron P. Bernstein/Getty Images; 17, ©Chip Somodevilla/Getty Images; 19, ©Win McNamee/Getty Images; 21, ©Alex Wong/Getty Images; 22, ©Mario Tama/Getty Images; 23, ©Junial Enterprises/Shutterstock; 23, ©Rido/Shutterstock; 23, ©Mondadori Portfolio/Getty Images; 23, ©The Toidi/Shutterstock

Library of Congress Cataloging-in-Publication Data

Names: Rose, Rachel, 1968- author.
Title: Kamala Harris : first female vice president / Rachel Rose.
Description: Minneapolis, Minnesota : Bearport Publishing Company, 2021. |
Series: Bearcub bios | Includes bibliographical references and index.
Identifiers: LCCN 2020058671 (print) | LCCN 2020058672 (ebook) | ISBN 9781636913278 (library binding) | ISBN 9781636913285 (paperback) | ISBN 9781636913292 (ebook)
Subjects: LCSH: Harris, Kamala, 1964---Juvenile literature. | Vice-Presidents--United States--Biography--Juvenile literature. | Women legislators--United States--Biography--Juvenile literature. | African American women legislators--Biography--Juvenile literature.
Classification: LCC E901.1.H37 R67 2021 (print) | LCC E901.1.H37 (ebook) | DDC 973.934092 [B]--dc23 LC record available at https://lccn.loc.gov/2020058671LC ebook record available at https://lccn.loc.gov/2020058672

For more information, write to Bearport Publishing, 5357 Penn Avenue South, Minneapolis, MN 55419. Printed in the United States of America.

Contents

Vice President 4

Kamala's Life 6

Did You Know? 22

Glossary 23

Index 24

Read More 24

Learn More Online 24

About the Author 24

Kamala Harris had a big smile.

She learned she would be **vice president**.

Kamala was the first woman to get the job.

5

Kamala's Life

Kamala was born in California.

But her parents were not from the United States.

Her mother was from India.

Kamala's father was born in Jamaica.

Kamala's home
in California

Ever since she was little, Kamala wanted to help people.

She knew she wanted to be a **lawyer**.

So, Kamala worked hard in school.

Kamala went to
school here.

Her hard work paid off.

Kamala became a lawyer in California.

She kept working hard to help kids.

Kamala cared about having good schools.

Kamala's jobs got bigger.

After a while, she was the top lawyer in California.

Kamala spent years
making sure people
followed laws.

Then, she wanted to help
make the laws.

She was **voted** into the
U.S. **Senate** in 2017.

Kamala was **proud** of what she had done.

She made laws to help everyone.

But she knew she could still do more.

NATIONAL ACTION NETWORK
Founded 1991
NO JUSTICE NO PEACE
NATIONAL ACTION
NAN
Founded 1991
TICE, NO
AL ACTION
NAL ACTIO

In 2019, Kamala tried to become president.

That did not happen.

But Joe Biden picked her to be vice president.

Joe Biden

In 2021, Kamala started her new job.

She still works hard for others.

Kamala wants everyone to have a good life.

Did You Know?

Born: October 20, 1964

Family: Shyamala (mother), Donald (father), Maya (sister)

When she was a kid: She visited India with her mother and her sister.

Special Fact: Kamala wrote a picture book. It is called *Superheroes Are Everywhere*.

Kamala says: "You're a hero by being the very best you."

Life Connections

Kamala cares about people. She works hard to help them. What do you do to show someone that you care?

Glossary

lawyer a person whose job it is to help others with law problems

proud very happy because of something you have or have done

Senate a part of the U.S. government that makes laws

vice president a person who is second in charge after the president

voted picked by a group who agreed on something

Index

California 6–7, 10, 12

India 6, 22

Jamaica 6

jobs 4, 12, 20

laws 14, 16

lawyer 8, 10, 12

Senate 14

vice president 4, 18

Read More

Murray, Julie. *Vice President (My Government).* Minneapolis: Abdo, 2018.

Susienka, Kristen. *Kamala Harris (African American Leaders of Courage).* New York: PowerKids Press, 2020.

Learn More Online

1. Go to **www.factsurfer.com**
2. Enter "**Kamala Harris**" into the search box.
3. Click on the cover of this book to see a list of websites.

About the Author

Rachel Rose is a writer who lives in San Francisco. Her favorite books to write are those about people who lead inspiring lives.